J.N. Nicholas

Brass:
the hunter

**A Brass Rivers Adventure,
Introducing US Deputy Marshal,
Brass Rivers**

J.N. Nicholas

www.baobabtreebooks.com
www.brassrivers.com

ISBN – 978-1-909389-01-4

This book series is based on Bass Reeves (July 1838 – 12 January 1910), possibly the first African American to receive a commission as a Deputy US Marshal.

Brass: the hunter

J.N. Nicholas

PROLOGUE

Standing under the shade of the wooden shack's overhang on a small veranda, Candace shields her eyes from the noonday sun, staring into the distance at a lone rider slowly moving behind a wall of dust, towards the house.

Brushing aside a long lock of twisted, natural hair, she smiles. Her wide mouth moves easily across her oval face while tan eyes brighten above high cheekbones. Straightening a stained apron around a simple blue cotton dress she hopes she is presentable for the man bent over in his saddle, plodding ever closer.

Darting inside she runs through the simple dining area, its large unlit fireplace blackened with soot while the wooden dining table with its two accompany chairs is decorated with a laced tablecloth and smart silver utensils. Heading into the bedroom to the right, a cracked mirror is erected by one wall. Posing, she spins looking at her figure, nodding with approval at what she sees. Hitching her skirt hem high to her upper thighs, she stares at the reflection of her long, strong, brown, shapely legs. She smiles again. *He'll like*, she says aloud, laughing.

Smoothing the dress and apron they mould, accentuating her curves - waist, buttocks and bosom. A chapped hand, garnered from years of homely chores, cups each breast. Closing her eyes she feels his big hands caressing them, gently massaging, pinching, playing. A bigger grin spreads over her attractive face. Her lips quiver as she runs her slim tongue over them.

She's glad her hero is home.

1

The bartender holds a clear glass in one hand while in the other he uses a once-white rag to give it more shine. A grimace on his narrow face suggests he isn't winning.

About to spit, he refrains as a stranger enters through the saloon's bat wing doors. They flap.

The shadow of a falling sun allows the man's silhouette to stretch along the wooden dusty floor. Head bent, his Stetson hides his face as he strikes a match against the thigh of his faded denim's. Without raising his head he puts the light to a custom-made cigarette protruding from his thick lips and inhales. A stream of grey smoke lazily swirls towards the ceiling, disappearing in the sticky air. The handle-bar moustache descending on both sides of his lips, quivers. Under his weather-beaten, once brown coat, a dirty white shirt covers his broad chest. A single gun is strapped high on his right hip. The belt filled with unused bullets.

Silence befalls the few patrons dotted around the saloon, their once busy chatter overtaken by the presence of the tall man.

Slowly he walks to the ornate bar, spurs jangling as they make a rhythmic *clanging* tune.

From one end of the room to the next a huge mirror provides a reflective backdrop to the elongated bar and the saloon. Varying rows of alcohol bottles line the wooden shelves - from the cheapest rotgut whiskey to the most expensive champagne - displayed in front of it.

Nervously, rubbing his hands in the messy apron tied around his obese waist, the bartender tries to smile. He fails. His heavy jowls hindering any attempt to make him look genuine.

"Can ah help you misstah?" He drawls. Black stained teeth match unwelcoming beady eyes.

"Maybe," Head bowed, the man inhales before answering. "Shot of whiskey wood bi nice."

The bartender reaches for a deep brown bottle and unscrews the cap. He pours the liquid into a tumbler and leaves the bottle unopened on the bar, "New in town?"

The guest doesn't look at the bartender, "Maybe."

Throwing his head back the man downs the liquid in one gulp and sputters. The sour burning sensation tastes good. Taking the bottle, he pours some more.

The bartender gasps on seeing his face; staggering, his mouth working as if to speak. Finally he finds his voice, "We...we don't serve your kin' inn here."

The man pauses and stares over the edge of his glass, dark eyes studying the cowering man behind the counter.

"Han what kind mite that be, Mistah? I figure hafftah ah long ride, ah man his entitled tah ah drink. So's can drink where I please, I reckon. Ain't that so?"

Groping for something to say the bartender looks relieved as he hears chairs behind the stranger scrape the bare floorboards.

"Get tha shit outtah here niggah, yah heard the barkeep."

Sighing, the stranger places the half empty glass slowly onto the bar before turning to view the speaker.

Standing a few feet away, two men; one heavy set, sweating profusely, an unlit cigar juts from his fat face while a hand hovers above his gun. The other, slimmer, gun low on his side, dressed entirely in black, stares, a hard unflinching blue gaze at the stranger. Thin lips pressed together giving nothing away.

The fat one speaks again, "Get tha shit outtah here niggah. Ain't telling you again."

Easing from the bar the stranger gently speaks, "Lissen gents, ah've been in tha saddle for days. All ah want is ah peaceful drink. No trouble. Juss ah drink, then ah'm on mah way, friend."

"We don't give ah shit. Get tha shit out," the fat man snarls. "Yah know niggah, tha thing is do yah want tah walk or be carried out? Your choice?"

The stranger adjusts his leather gloves, one after the other, "Lissen friend, yah know that's tha third time yah called me niggah." He pauses, almost murmuring, "Ah hate been called niggah."

"Ah don't give ah dog's crutch what yah like or don't like niggah, yah need tah go now," The stout man moves closer and almost in touching distance, he makes to grab the man by his lapels.

The stranger sidesteps, clutching the big man's hand as he goes. Tugging him to one side, the fat man loses his balance and staggers howling, crashing into the bar with a heavy thud. The other patron's duck behind their tables watching the scenario unfold.

From his periphery the tall man sees the hand of the slimmer one dip. Instinctively he dives to his right, a gun suddenly appearing in his hand. Hitting the floor, he fans the hammer. Dust clouds plume as lands. He coughs but it doesn't affect his aim. The slim man returns fire. His shots smack the bar where he once stood, the projectiles making 'thud' sounds into the wood. The Black Man fires twice more into the slimmer man and watches as he lurches, a wry smile emerging on the dying man's narrow face, for a moment he teeters before dropping.

The stranger wastes no time watching him fall and rolls onto one knee, facing the man's friend again. The man writhes in pain, the force of being thrown into the bar cracking a rib or two. The patrons stand tentatively and walk slowly over.

"Shit Bob, he got Jake real good," pipes one man.

The fat man screams, "Why yah shitting niggah, yah broke mah ribs and killed mah gud friend!"

Re-holstering his gun the outsider stands walks over to the bar and sighs again before lifting the tumbler to his lips, "Ah told yah friend, all ah wanted was ah quiet drink."

On his back like a cow about to be branded, the man claws for his weapon. He roars, "Why yah little shit!"

Stepping away from the bar the man's gun is in his hand before the fat one can grip his, "Don't be ah fool friend, live ah bit longer while yah can."

"Why yah...," there's a resigned look on the man's face and he struggles unsteadily to his feet brushing aside helping hands. "Get off me, yah shits and you...yah killed my friend!"

Someone says, "Ah never seen ah man draw ah gun soh fast Joe. Lissen toh him, leave him, he had yah dead tah rites."

Finishing his drink the stranger wipes his mouth with the back of a dirty glove, "Lissen tah yah friend, friend. As fah yah dead friend ovah there, he was better than you fah one and two, he was about tah kill me. Couldn't allow that tah happen."

The fat man moans, lurching to where his friend lays dead. Three congealing bullet holes placed neatly in his chest; another hole is in the centre of his forehead.

"Yah shit!" He growls and clutches his gun, cheeks flushed bright pink.

Finishing the bottle the Black man tosses two dollar coins onto the bar and looks at the bartender, "For tha drink..."

Adjusting his ankle length coat he relights another roll-up and heads to the door, "...tha rest fah cleaning up tha two men who messed up yah floor."

The bartender splutters, "Two men...there's only o..."

With another roar the fatter man pulls his gun but before it clears leather, the first bullet rips into his heart. A second sinks into his gun hand and spinning, he slams into the tables and chairs, dropping to the floor. Dead.

Crouching by the door smoke curling from his gun the visitor straightens, spitting out his cigarette, "Like ah said…two men."

Feeling his way around the bar, the barkeep sways to the two bodies staining his wooden floor. The murmuring customers rising from their concealed positions.

"Who tha shit are yah, yah bastard?" Someone asks.

The man cracks a cold smile, revealing pristine white teeth, "Ah was once ah slave. Call me anything else but niggah." He pauses, digging around in his pockets, "next time yah'all will think before calling someone like me niggah again."

Finding another cigarette he lights it, "Good day tah yah sirs."

Tipping the edge of his hat in salutation, he walks into the early evening sunshine and its suffocating heat.

2

A grey wisp of smoke floats skywards, vanishing into the blackness. The dying embers signal a fire nearing the end of its life. Overhead stars flicker on and off as they play games in the heavens.

Using a stick, Toledo Jones stokes the dying ashes. They spark into life, briefly flickering flashes in his flat eyes. A wry smile dances on his thick lips.

A man walks into the little light left by the fire, "Comanche Cole says tha Sheriff'll be outtah town...."

Toledo grunts.

"...says we can move by morning."

Toledo says nothing and eases from his hunches to be on his back. Unhitching his gun belt he removes his gun, placing it under a bedroll –

the pillow for his head. Taking his hat, he covers his face.

Behind his eyes, a previous life emerges in sharp images. A laughing little boy aged about ten, runs towards a river and without stopping, dives in ans water splashes as if someone tossed in a large rock. The little boy vanishes under the swirling stream.

"We move hat dawn. Tell tha men tha money in that bank is hours," His voice muffles. The man nods, not that Toledo cares he's staring at the river. He never sees the little boy again.

Sheriff Jim Davis glances at a large map on his desk. An hour-glass shade lamp burns a yellowy-gold flame, its blaze dances across the paper. A Winchester repeating rifle is across the scratched desktop; joining a few wanted posters, a tin cup empty of coffee and a tin plate half-filled with beans and a chunk of bread.

He takes a stubby finger, jabbing at a trail running through the map while looking at the men around the table. Nobody speaks.

"Tha last report we had, says he and his gang are 'long here sumwhere".

"So we split up?" A heavy-set man asks.

Sheriff Davis breaks a piece of bread, chewing around a wad before answering, "Tha best way."

Silence descends upon the group. The ten heavily armed men digest the earlier news they received, telegraphed across the state. The residents of San Antonio had felt the wrath and enterprise of The Toledo Jones Gang and their warning was stark – *get the Toledo Gang before they get to you.*

"What about the town Sheriff, who we leaving?"

"That'll be you Wade, Terrence and Clayton. Mr. Thompson, Mr. Carlson and Mr. Brevitt will also help out." The last three men, local merchants.

"Awright, we leave in four hours, at tha break of dawn," He pauses, "make sure yo're supplied. We may be out thare for ah few days."

Spurs clink on the floorboards as the men depart from the small room. A few walked to grab some shut-eye in empty cells while a couple rest on their blankets placed on the floor.

Light coloured clouds emerge from over the horizon; dawn's relentless approach is near.

Sheriff Davis rolls up the chart and stuffs it into a saddlebag. Sitting in an old leather chair, he kicks his feet onto the desk, placing the rifle over his lap. Pulling a hat over his face, he falls immediately asleep.

Just before losing consciousness, he muses, "Toledo Jones, ain't shit."

3

Watching Candace bend over the lip of the bricked well, drawing water, he smiled. Last night was as great as every night. The way she massaged his tense shoulders and ran her fingers along the spine of his back, he knew he had married the right woman. Pausing and flexing his tired muscles, he placed down the axe; there was enough wood for the fireplace now. Staring at his wife, he felt the stirring return to his loins and sitting on a rickety chair by the door, he stared at her as if caught in awe. The green backdrop behind the shapely figure like a landscaped painting. There was one such mural in his Colonel's quarter, he remembered; hanging from cord, nailed to a wooden wall. She straightened. Locks waving. 'She is so beautiful,' he mused...

Astride his mustang, the Marshal surveys the sprawling vegetation. Rising east to west like an undulating river were the Ouachita Mountains with it blotches of grey strata interrupting the sequence, indicating the rocks had something to say about the land. To the south was Hot Springs - a smaller town and directly west - Little Rock.

The Marshal pats the horse's neck, drawling, "Well girl looks like another day on the trail."

Blaze snorts and staring at the ground the Marshal scrutinises the earth for any sign. A path of squashed grass leads into a valley of oak, hickory and pine trees.

"Sumbuddy came this way awright." Sneaking a roll-up from a denim pocket, he puts it to his lips; deliberately he strikes a match against his thigh - it sputters to life. Dragging on his makeshift cigarette he nudges the mare forward. She trudges down the slope and into valley, following the trail.

Tapping his pocket, he feels the tin badge against his chest. Since the war had ended all he ever wished for was to sit on his veranda, his beautiful wife beside him, staring across the plain and watching the waist high common grass dance in the warm breeze. He smiles. The thought of her on the wooden bench makes him hanker for her touch even more but the newly appointed US Marshal James F. Fagan gave him no choice when he came a-calling; there was a favour needed repaying.

Zigzagging, avoiding low hanging branches, he swears, wishing he had never taken part in that damn civil war.

The group of men are in no hurry as they allow their rides to amble through shrub. Hooves clomp on the ground and long limbered legs swish against troubled brush while darkness cloaks the land, the sun yet to reveal its hot face. Nobody says anything, their minds on the riches hidden in Springdale Central Bank. A spur jangles, its noise carrying in the night.

"Quiet!" hisses Toledo Jones, "We're near tha town. Comanche...scout ahead will yah. See how tha land lies...tha rest ah yah, stay put."

The gang rein in, alighting from their mounts and stretching their tired legs. The smell of perspiration emanates from them like a smelly pit latrine. A few check their weapons and hammer click as soundless barrels spin are greeted with grunts of satisfaction. The remaining men roll out their bedrolls and ready to bed down for the night. It will be a while before Comanche Cole returns.

Their horses are at full gallop as Sheriff Davis and his posse storm into the morning. The tip they received from an Indian said the Toledo Jones

Gang were about seventy miles south, bedded down in Savannah Canyon – a box canyon with a small stream filtering through the hard packed dirt floor. *We need to catch this vermin before he moves,* he muses. The crescendo of horse hooves sounding like thunder in his ears as sweat gathers in his eyes and he swipes at it with the back of a gloved hand. In the next ten miles they'll have to stop and proceed quietly.

A poncho covers a squat Comanche Cole; his eyes narrow, hidden by a large sombrero while he studies Main Street. Sitting under an overhang, lost in the shadows cast by the rising sun, he grins. The black night having given way sees merchants sweeping their stoops and hailing each other *'good morning'*. So innocent. So naïve.

A fat man, wearing a grey bowler hat, black waistcoat and cream-coloured pants waddles into view. He looks out of place, better suited for the East, as he saunters to the bank's glass panelled doors and unlocks it before entering. A wry smile plays on the outlaw's lips and walking unhurriedly heads to the rear of a vacant building.

4

Water dripped from her shiny, dark chocolate complexion, pooling at her barefeet. Behind her, even the lake seemed captivated by her presence, its blueness barely moving like someone holding their breath. He knew he was, the nakedness of the woman before him squeezing his insides, forcing him to dream about being submerged within her wholesomeness. Turning to face him, she caught his eyes and laughed. He grinned. If he wasn't mistaken, she sounded like a sweet-singing morning jay.

Trotting their mounts nonchalantly up Main Street, dust devil whiff upwards. Heavy set, dirty and grey from the trails grime, kerchiefs cover the lower half of the men's faces. A woman glances in their direction and scampers into the nearest shop. Shortly after a man emerges and quickly walks towards the Sheriff's Office, glimpsing frantically over his shoulder in the direction of the heavily armed men while mopping his brow with a silken kerchief.

Toledo smiles unhitching the thin leather strap securing his gun. "Let's move! Joe, you and Will set up ova thare," He points to a stack of barrels facing the main street town buildings, "Frank, you, Ruez and Comanche head ova thare."

Toledo points to the opposite side of the wide street; the men scurrying to their positions.

"Pat, Jack, Juaniez and Billy, yah know what tah do." They draw their guns and readjusting their face kerchief masks, rush to the Bank. Toledo follows as the doors splinter under the weight of a kicked boot.

Someone yells, "Don't move fatso! This is a hold up! Yah holler, it'll be tha last thing yah do!"

It takes a few minutes for the realisation to creep up on him and the man stifles a scream, eventually jabbering as he suddenly finds his voice.

"Don't kill me! Please, don't kill me!"

Toledo enters, stepping over the door debris just as Pat slaps the fat banker's face. It shakes, quivering like the man standing in front of the grilled counter.

"Where's tha loot?"

A darkening stain swells at the front of the banker's pants. He stutters, "P...Please don't...don't kill me."

Pat snarls, grabbing the man's shirt, hauling him on his toes, "Don't let me ask agin...open tha shiting safe!"

A heavy shove sends the man sprawling to the rear of the room and he lands heavily before a large black steel door.

Peeling a strip from a dried tobacco stem, Toledo pops it into his mouth and begins to chew. Strolling to a bench he sits on the bench used for waiting customers. Gnawing, saying nothing, he toys with his gun, cold eyes watching the scene unfold.

"Hurry!" He hears Jack hiss. "We don't have all day."

There's another slap. The banker wails, stubby fingers feeling his face while fingering the safes dial. There's a loud *clunk* as the lock engages and the safes door swings open.

"Mama!"

Toledo smirks and stands stretching. *Juaniez and his bloody mother!* He knew there was no better time than the present to rob the bank.

The information he had gleaned from Laura, his telegraph lover in Fayetteville, some nights ago. She assured him a US Army unit would be escorting some forty thousand dollars from Springdale to Fort Smith within two days. The vast sums of money acquired from merchant takings at the nearby silver mine. He smiles tickling an itch in his crotch; a reminder of what kind of reward she would receive when he next visits.

Light brown sacks with dark *Springdale Central Bank* markings on the sides and tied with a leather thong are stacked on four shelves. Pushing the bulbous man aside, two of the men grab them before handing over to the other two. In a matter of minutes they hold the safes ten bags.

Juaniez turns to Toledo, "Ready..."

Suddenly a salvo of shots echo from the street and striding to the open door he looks out quickly assessing the situation.

He sees the Sheriff's deputies caught in his crossfire; two bullet-riddled bodies are on the rutted road, their blood soiling the earth. To his left, a number of men trade shots with Frank and Comanche Cole returning fire while Ruez sits as if enjoying the mayhem; a red blotch tarnishing his dirty-white shirt front.

Inside the bank, Toledo indicates the men to the door gesturing with his head. They rush out, firing as they go.

The banker, in one corner, whimpers as he cowers. his eyes pleading, lips trembling. Taking a step towards him Toledo fires, the bullet smashing into the man's chest. The whimpering ends.

Running outside, Toledo grabs his unsettled horse's reins and leaps into the saddle, shouting, "Let's go!"

Bullets chip the ground and the slipstream of one whispers by his face. He returns fire at the crouched men and stupidly Mr Carlson, shotgun in hand, attempts to run across the street.

Without aiming while fighting his bucking mount, Toledo fans his guns hammer. It kicks twice. Mr Carlson pitches; a bullet slamming into his side, the other smashes into his head, crashing to the ground, he twitches before lying still.

"Yah!" Throwing his weight, Toledo drives his speckled brown steed up the street. There's no need to look behind since he knows his men are already following his example.

5

The barren ground was bare of any vegetation and like the naked or half naked bodies dotted across it, parts were of them were bloated with a myriad of bleak colours; black crater holes and gnarled, naked trees carry the battlefield scars. He crawled into a ditch. It was deep. The still, stagnant water smelt like the air around him with the fresh blood odour and burnt flesh clogging his nostrils. He puked. Closely his eyes, his head sunk to the earth, settling in the muddy, brackish water.

"Who's dead?" Sheriff Davis asks. A glassy stare falls on the four covered bodies on the sidewalk boards, "How tha shit did they get into town without us knowing?"

He already knew the answer since Wade furnished a report as soon as he had returned.

Seated on a creaky chair behind a worn and creaky desk, Sheriff Davis curses the ground Toledo Jones and the men who followed him, walked on. Grabbing a bottle of rotgut whiskey, he puts the neck to his lips and swallows the liquid in large gulps. *Ah don't need this shit. How tha shit is this going to help me become Town Mayor? That damn shit!*

"What now Sheriff?" It's Terrence, fresh face having difficulty in hiding his anger mixed with fear, "We can still get 'em. Their tracks are still fresh."

Sheriff Davis liked Terrence, his enthusiasm contagious as well as dangerous, "Yo're right boy."

He stands unsteadily, the posse silent as they watch him, "Let's go hafttah them right now. Let's pursue this murdering shit this minute and get him for tha death of our friends."

Walking over to Ruez's prone body, he heaves a massive kick into the wrapped corpse, "Those pieces of shit will die Terrence. Believe me, they will." He takes another swig from the bottle, "Who's willing tah ride tonight?"

Otherwise than his remaining nodding deputies, the others look away.

"Am not sure Sheriff; ah have mah family tah think about." One man mumbles.

Another says, "We would love to follow Sheriff but what happens if they return? Who'll be here?"

A next man murmurs, "It didn't help your deputies or Mr Carlson none."

Sheriff Davis stumbles and looks at the men gathered in his small office, "Who the hell said that?" Nobody owns up. "Well? Yah shits! Cowards! Yah know what...get tha shit outtah mah office."

Unexpectedly, he throws the bottle onto the far wall and they all watch it shatter, its contents splattering over them while they filed out one-by-one.

Travelling quickly over the heavily wooded Ouachita Mountains and towards the Boston Mountains, the Marshal stands by Arkansas River's edge. Water gurgles, flowing south, a wall of green stretching along both banks. Many miles to the northeast lay Clarkesville - another small town suddenly springing from the wild western wilderness. To the west, at least a days ride away, Fort Smith - providing security for far-flung residents.

Bending towards the water, he fills his canteens with the cool liquid while beside him Blaze laps the precious fuel, pink tongue darting in and out of the water like a wild toad's. High above, pine trees reach for the intermittent blue sky as it battles through the trees thick leaves. It's cool under the vast emerald ceiling yet he sweats profusely.

Releasing the saddle's cinch and girth, he struggles with it to the root of a pine tree before returning to Blaze and removing the blanket from the mare's back, he pats her down.

"Looks like we have ah few days more Blaze. Wonder where they're hat now?"

His horse ignores him and continues munching strands of grass.

"Ignore me won'tcha, jus' like Candace would," He laughs lightly, adjusting the bedroll. Using his saddle as a pillow he places his gun under the covers, almost falling onto the makeshift bed, sleep consumes him. As he closes his eyes a feeling of remorse invades him. Candace. *How could ah jus' leave? Why did ah leave? For tha job? How long has it been, will ah ever go back? Will she be there when ah return?*

Placing his hat over his face he hides from the peeping sunbeams. *Candace.*

The sound of a woodpecker hammering monotonously at some tree pushes him into oblivion while the image of the woman he still loves floats into dreamy view.

He isn't sure what awakes him but his Creek Indian upbringing thrust itself into his consciousness. Prone, he listens, distinguishing the wood's different sounds. High in the treetops, pine warblers croon and trudging somewhere nearby, a herd of white-tailed deer, moan deeply. Blaze's ears prick, flicking frequently before training in one direction.

The Marshal stares to where she faces and listens. A stealthy step, nothing like an animal's, muffled and yet audible, caresses his ears. Gripping his gun he gently eases back the hammer, placing his finger on the trigger.

A man emerges from the brush wearing a poncho. He moves softly, a large sombrero pushed back on his dark hair. A knife glints in one hand, its steely sheen flickering once in the sunlight's sporadic beam. He recognises the man's weather-beaten, shrivelled face from the wanted poster in his saddlebag - long nose, round chin, squinting eyes, permanent sneer. *Comanche Cole!*

With minimum movement, the Marshal releases his gun and clutches the handle of his knife in his waist sheath.

Crouching, Cole advances, a shaft of sunlight hitting his knife again. It glints wickedly. Reaching the Marshal he pauses and raises his knife arm; suddenly he swings.

The Marshal rolls into his legs, catching him off-guard and Cole drops heavily over his body. Dancing to his feet, the Marshal turns bent at the knees and facing Cole, balances his knife lightly in one big hand.

"Yuh die today stranger, eh?" The Cole mutters, catching sight of the Marshal's badge, "Ah Lawman eh?"

The Marshal nods, "Yah Cole. Fo sure one of us will be dead today and tha other will jus' walk away."

The Indian starts, the corner of one eye twitching. "Soh yuh know me eh..."

Leaping forward, a cold triumphant grin set on his hard face, he swings his knife again. The Marshal feints, leaping back, one foot catches a pine branch knurling from the earth and he falls. Cole seizes the chance, diving towards him, "Yuh time tah die Negro..."

His knife hand drives for the Marshal's chest who rolls again and Cole's knife plunges into the soft earth. Throwing a boot, the Marshal connects with the outlaw's side; Cole grunts and he rolls away.

Both men bounce to their feet circling each other like the buzzards high above the trees. Their heavy laboured breathing, the only noise in the quiet forest.

"A Negro as a Lawman, shit," Cole coaxes, "com'on Marshall, take me."

"That's what ah said tah yah Ma las' night Cole."

The Indian explodes and lunges, arm extended. The Marshal dodges deftly, hitting his knife hand up and away and swings his own. There's a *thud*. Cole stiffens and perches on his moccasin toes, a glazed look creeping into his stunned eyes , slowly they roll into his head.

"Shit Negro..." He sighs, crumpling to the grassy ground. A complete silence descends on the forest floor. Wiping his knife clean on the dead man's poncho, the Marshal muses, "About yah mother Cole...ah was only joking but at least yah didn't say niggah."

Sheriff Davis checks his shotgun. Unhitching his steed, he waits for the other two men to mount, another two men stand on the covered sidewalk. He couldn't leave the town unsecured, so his two best deputies will have to do. *Tha shits! Leaving me with two good men tah follow ah murderous gang.*

He stares at the audience in front of his Office: *Tha good and great of Springdale, tha shits!* Spitting into the dirt and without a word he slaps his spurs into the horse's flanks, she snorts and turns before galloping suddenly up Main Street.

#

They talked about having children but it never happened, especially with the war creeping, state by state. She cried. He cried. They argued. Made love. In the end he went. Anyway. Riding away he never looked back. He wished he had

Laura's slim naked, spotless body seems little and fragile in contrast to his larger battered and scarred one. Asleep, her chest heaves gently, head lodged in the crook of a thick bicep cushioning her blond hair

Since the Springdale job and distributing the loot amongst the men, he advised them to lie low and out of state; a few went to Louisiana - to the south, and two to Texas - in the southwest. Nobody wished to enter

Oklahoma which was to the west; with the gang's reputation well known throughout, their faces plastered throughout the state.

Toledo sucks on a cigarette before expelling smoke. Watching a ring float to the ceiling, he smiles. Missouri to the north, Tennessee and Mississippi in the east were still untapped. *Next stop Missouri then Texas.*

A light tap on the room door disturbs him and he bawls to the unseen visitor, "Who tha shit...this better be good!"

He hates being disturbed after days in the saddle, worse when a naked woman's by his side.

"Who tha shit is it?"

Laura stirs but fails to wake, her eyes closed and lost in the bliss created in her mind.

Easing her from his arm Toledo grabs his gun and he walks naked to the door, cigarette between his teeth, "Ah said who tha shit is it?"

"It's me boss." *Will.*

Toledo grunts, for any of his men to bother him it must be important. Opening the door, wide eyes on a freckled face stares at him.

"Boss Comanche's dead."

Toledo says nothing but stare hard at the bearer of bad news and removing the cigarette, he whispers, "How'd it happ'n?"

Comanche Cole, one of the few men he liked. A full-blooded Comanche, Cole found his way into Arkansas after his tribes skirmishes with the US Army in north-western Texas. He hated the thought of being imprisoned on a reservation where his people were forced to live. A small area on rocky ground, too tough to farm, too hard to graze. Filled with hate, he went on a violent rampage before making good his escape to Monroe, North Louisiana, where he and Toleedo met in a bar-room fight. Someone had made the mistake of insulting Cole - him being an Indian - and Toledo being Toledo, didn't like the odds. Five men died that night. If there was one thing Toledo liked about Comanche Cole was his dependability and loyalty, and he was a good man with a knife.

The young man, head bowed, murmurs, "Don't know boss, he was tied tah his horse. Word came from Clarksville there was ah note on him."

"Wha' did it say?"

"Wasn't clear boss, som'thing about the body bein' Comanche Cole and signed USDM."

"USDM, US Marshal?"

"Yeah boss. No name?"

"No name."

Laura rolls and Toledo, smiles coldly. Leering at her nakedness, he scratches at his crotch. Last night was good like the so many other nights, the so many other women, in so many other towns. Adorning his clothes, he adjusts his gun-belt and using a leather throng, ties the holster low-down on one thigh.

"Who else with yah?" He growls.

"Frank and Pat are outside. Joe, Jack, Juan and Billy are outtah state."

"K." Toledo slaps a dirty Stetson onto his oily hair. His bushy eyebrows furrow and craggy lines at the corners of his eyes and mouth crack even longer. His dark skin glistens with perspiration and using a dirty towel wipes his face. Glancing at Laura again, he grins, her soft breath is lost in the musty air.

"Get word tah tha rest."

Will nods, knowing better than to ask how that can be done. Toledo sets his mouth and says nothing while walking from the room, Will following.

Large dollops of rain touch the Marshal's hat brim evaporating into his clothes, rolling down his saddle and along Blaze's back. The ground is slushy with the water. Unfurling a poncho curled from his saddlebag, he puts it on, pulling his hat over his face, trying to hide from the deluge. It comes down in buckets.

"Well Blaze 'nother wet day tah deal with." Blaze plods, hooves squishing and squashing wild clumps of Bermuda grass. "Yup another wet day."

Tugging the cloak closer and hunching his shoulders, he settles further into his covering.

Toledo gnaws the end of his cigarette, his thick fingers caressing the six-shooters walnut handle. He didn't like the thought of Comanche Cole being dead – *was there an assassin or bounty hunter on their tail?* Gritting his teeth, he snips the cigar's end off and lets it fall to the ground.

Pulling the reins, he leads the group through the town of Fayetteville; Main Street is quiet. The suns long gone as the smell of horse manure mixes with pine wood fires and permeates in the air. The sound of a clinking piano accompanied by raucous singing and tinkle of glass comes from the *Fayetteville Saloon* while it lamps illuminate the dirt-laden street by leaving the window's bright square emblazoned on the ground.

Toledo looks at the men riding behind him, even in the evening's dusk he sees dust rising rising from the horse's hoofs. He nods.

The freckled face Will, the boy he rescued from a previous employer - a steer drover for the YT Ranch, somewhere near Jonesboro. And who he shot dead as he was about to whip the then young boy. It was a good thing Toledo rode into town as he was about to lift the whip for the umpteenth time. He shakes his head, young Will would probably be dead, if he hadn't stepped in. *And all the yellow-bellied townsfolk did was watch;* from then on, Young Will never left his side.

He looked at the former Rebel Army colleagues, Frank and Pat. Former riders with the infamous Quantrill Raiders, They hated life after the war and continued killing Union now US Army soldiers and with the bounty on their head multiplying with each murder, they were constantly on the move. It was while Toledo was in the process of robbing a bank in Richmond when they came across him, helping him to finish off the robbery, murder a few people, escape and share in the loot.

A long scar - the wound from a Union sabre - stuck to Pat's long face and solemn eyes hid the blanket of cruelty within him. Frank, shorter of the two, fidgeted consistently with the bullets in his belt; taking out each one before replacing into a different hole - a mindless and senseless habit.

He breaks their quiet while they sat on the hard ground, clear of the town's boundary The suffocating smell of the day is replaced by the forest's crisp air, arguing crickets, hooting owls and faraway a howling coyote howls.

"We know who did this boss?" He drawls.

"Ah can think of a number of people Frank but this one left a note."

The men are still again. The sound of their snorting horses and clomping hooves on the worn track, the only noises. A whitish-yellow moon peeps above The Ozarks, stretching the shadows from inanimate and animate objects. Off to the south, a wall of pine trees cast a line of blackness and a few times, glowering stares of some unknown animal, peeps from the gloom.

"Where was he last Will?" Toledo asks.

"The guy told me somewhere in between Fort Smith and Clarksville."

"Ok we start at Fort Smith. We're looking for a Deputy US Marshal," He pulls at his horse's reins, barking, "let's ride!"

7

Candace smiled. He loved the way she looked, hips swaying as she walked toward the fireplace. A large steel pot steamed over open flames, its yellowish orange fire moving against the pot's blackened sides. Using a deep wooden ladle, she fished out lentil soup and poured it into a bowl. Within a few paces she was back by his side, the hot brew before him. Gently she kissed his forehead. "Here you are baby."

He grinned roping an arm around her hips. He was happy, she was happy.

The rain surrenders to yellow beams of sunlight penetrating through the thick pine foliage and grass twits call while Blaze stomps through the woods. The Marshal chews beef jerky and drinks from a canteen. He has no time to stop and set up camp.

"You know Blaze, chas'n this bloody Toledo Gang throughout the territories is one tiring shit. When will he stop just long enuff for us to get him?" Fort Smith is still half a days ride away.

Dew glistens across the open land as they trot across it and in the distance, the tall pine trees are dark, contrasting sharply with the blue sky speckled with its white clouds. A Red deer darts from the undergrowth and setting its long head stares at him and horse before hastily returning to its hiding place.

The Marshal grins, *Candace would've love this,* he muses. He knows that with the woods being still, the distant croaking of restless frogs and creaking crickets; would've made her smile. He wonders what she's doing - or who she could with; shaking the thought, he refocuses on the task at hand.

They once went to their special place just outside of Little Rock; open and green and as still as where he presently rides, they played in-between the trees and made love in the long grass. He sights a butterfly bouncing unerringly nearby and the sweet grass smell adds to the pine trees aroma.

He remembers holding her, arms wrapped about her with soft pine nettles acting as a makeshift bed, caressing her face as he gently kissed her soft lips...

...The clatter of wheels on rough ground interrupts him. Drawing Blaze's reins, he waits in the brush until the sound fades. He doesn't see the wagon but a horse's snort and quiet conversation between the wagon's driver and side-man float to where he hides in low-lying branches. Delicately, he kicks Blaze's flanks and steers her onto the path. Well-worn lines disappear in either direction and the fast settling dust indicates the carriage's route. It is heading to Fort Smith.

Sheriff Davis puts the canteen to his lips, taking a gulp, he wipes his forehead with a blue-chequered neck scarf. A bright film of sweat layers their horses and with heads bent, the animals lap water in long gulps. Everybody is stooping, filling canteens. At one stage they fill their hats and empty them over their dirty heads and soaking through their dusty clothes, cooling their nasty bodies.

Warren - a Deputy - stretches lazily on the hard ground. "Sheriff, we shou'd call in tho Marshals." He says, pulling a roll-up from a top pocket and lights the end. Grey smoke moves about him like early morning mist creeping across The Ozarks.

Sheriff Davis finishes patting down his steed and stares at his Deputy, "What?"

The second man, Percy is silent; his weathered, hard face gives nothing away. A wide black moustache hides his mouth and placing a hand on his rifle stock, he waits. The more senior of the two deputies he holds his breath, he knows Sheriff Davis only too well.

Sheriff Davis murmurs, "What you saying Warren? You speak like you don't want tah be here?"

"A'm juss saying Sheriff..."

"What did this prick do tah our town?"

"Sheriff we're out of our juris..."

Suddenly Sheriff Davis walks over, kicking Warren's feet away from under him. "You shit!"

Warren falls, screaming as another kick slams into his side. Rolling, he grunts, then staggering to his feet, another kick smashes into the side of his head. He drops heavily, blood springing like a newly-found spring after heavy rainfall.

Percy jumps hastily, placing himself in-between the Sheriff and his junior as he grabs onto his employer,

"Sheriff! Sheriff! What tha' shit you doing?"

Panting, Sheriff Davis fights him off, "If that shit wants the Marshals after this shitbag, he can go back to that rotten town of cowards and stay with them. Shit!"

Groaning, Warren is holding his bleeding head as blood seeps through his fingers. Pushing Sheriff Davis aside, Percy hurries and grabs his canteen. Splashing water onto Warren's wound and using his neck chief, he mops his friend's brow. Tipping Warren's head, he puts the canteen to his colleagues trembling lips.

"Ok...ok Sheriff," Warren mutters. "Sorry...I'm sorry, I just thought..."

Sheriff Davis says nothing and walks over to his horse. Mounting, he kicks it into a walk and is soon lost in the undergrowth.

A long, high wooden wall stands above the landscape - Fort Smith -

built by trees axed from the adjoining woods, it looks foreboding against the other dwellings dotted at its front. The fort acquired its name from General Thomas Adams Smith in the 1810's, who commanded the US Army Rifle Regiment, near St. Louis. In 1817, he ordered an Army topographical engineer, Stephen H. Long, to find a suitable site on the Arkansas River for a fort. Quickly helping to establish the homes and businesses of the early pioneers on its immediate outskirts, the fort eventually expanded into a thriving metropolis.

Blaze plods along the dusty trail heading into town. On both sides of the main thorough-fare, a wooden covered awning follows the wooded sidewalk; ending and beginning at a number of intersections. In the distance the walkway ends a few metres from the fort's exterior wall. Pedestrians troop along the sidewalk with most of the women townsfolk in high-necked blouses, frilly dresses, bonnets and hiding under pretty-patterned, frilly umbrellas. Amidst the chaos, wagons and riders on horseback kick up dust everywhere as they moved along the busy road. Midday noise from a saloon to the Marshal's left carries along the street, it draws his attention. *Cowboys having fun!* He smiles, licking his lips. He could do with a beer or some rotgut whiskey. Directing Blaze, he heads towards the din.

Three storeys high, the wooded façade of the saloon also housed a hotel, its many windows concealing nondescript rooms. Dismounting, he ties the reins against a wooden tie-post. Taking his hat off his head, he wipes sweat from his brow with the back of a gloved hand. Using it, he beats dust from his dusty clothes. The dust balloons, almost choking him. Dark perspiration stain his worn clothes and with its faded marks his dungarees, shows signs wear. Fixing the thick long coat about his shoulders he looks at the adjoining stores, noticing the towns people going about their business. Nothing seems untoward.

"Blaze, you stay rite here."

Hitching his gunbelt, he withdraws the Winchester from its scabbard and heads to Eddies *Emporium.* A portly man in a waistcoat stands behind a wooden counter and at his rear, numbered keys are in neat three rows. The hotelier eyes the Marshal suspiciously as he enters.

"No niggahs." He says.

Reaching the counter, the Marshal's eyes narrow but he ignores the man's quip. "Need ah room," he says.

The man repeats, "No niggahs."

The Marshal sighs, "Lissen, ah'm only going toh say this once. Ah'm going to the stable then will be back for ah room, if by then there's no room…"

He throws a few dollars on the counter and turns to leave.

"Ah said no niggahs you shit."

Without looking back the Marshal says nothing.

The stables are at the far end of the town and off to the right; it's empty of anyone but a few grazing nags. Leading Blaze, he finds an empty booth with mounds of hay strewn at the back. Removing the heavy saddle he pats her down with a wad of the hay.

"K, Blaze." She neighs, throwing her head back and forth before dipping it back into the hay. Grabbing his saddle, bags and blanket he returns to the hotel. Pushing through the glass doors without breaking stride, saddle stuff in hand, he walks directly over to the counter, leans across and grabs the hotelier by the throat, partially pulling him over the barrier.

"That room Eddie, now...one facing the street."

The man splutters, gagging, his hands tugging at the iron fists around his throat, "Ok...here....here..."

Roughly the Marshal thrusts him back, releasing his grip. Rubbing his throat, Eddie hands over a set of keys, "You...you'll be in Room 6, second floor."

Walking to a set of wooden stairs off from the counter, the Marshal's cold eyes bore into his ungracious host, "Good an so you know, the nex time if ah Marshal passes by make sure you're more polite....and if ah Blackman com's in here, *you* bettah be polite."

Dust devils dance when the hooves pound the main street into Fort Smith. Leading Toledo is followed by Will, Frank and Pat. The town is quiet with the only light coming from a spattering of oil lamps illuminating the night; the brightest set reflecting from the noisy saloon.

Will offers, "Ah sent a telegraph tah the guys, boss...they shou'd be here in a couple of days."

Toledo nods, munching on a cigar, "Let's head ova' tah the saloon. Will,

you and me start there. Frank, Pat
you go tah the hotel, ask around."

Loping to the rein stand, they lash
their horse's onto it and stroll
unhurriedly to rendezvous'.

8

The Marshal lies on his back, eyes closed, tiredness racking his weary body; the exertions against Comanche Cole adds to old wounds, aches and pains as they pound throughout his body. Sighing, his mind wonders to the prey of his current chase. *Where is he?* It didn't stay there and moved into a deeper haze. *Where is Candace now too? How is she? Will she even be there when I get back?* He sighs again, the thoughts too much to bear as darkness approached. *Ah need ah bath*, he whispers but before he moves to the large jug of water on the lone drawer, sleep overtakes him pulling him into its black chasm.

"Yuh shure this niggah's a Marshal?" Frank asks Eddie.

The hotelier rubs his throat reluctantly, "Yeah that's what he said, real hard case bastard, grabbed me by mah throat, nearly killed me."

"Where's that shithead niggah at now?"

Eddie points, "Upstairs, Room 6, second floor."

"He's the one all right?" Pat nods at Frank. "Ah'll get Toledo. You stay here Frank, watch if he comes down."

"Yeah," Frank pulls a gun from his holster, spinning the barrel, inserting a few bullets in empty chambers.

"Don't do anyting foolish Frank, I know how crazy yah can get."

"Yeah sure, sure. Ah'm crazy, jus' hurry back with Toledo."

Pat nods and leaves. Frank waits until he's gone before turning to Eddie, "Ah'm heading upstairs, killing this niggah myself."

Gun cocked, he tiptoes up the stairs, a few creak under his weight where he gingerly places one foot before the other.

The Marshal's eyes flutter open. Whatever snaps him from his reverie causes his nerves to tingle and clutching his gun, he rolls gently from the bed and onto the floor. Having the bed acting as a barrier, he stoops away from the door and waits.

The door buckles under Frank's kick and he enters fanning his gun's hammer, firing into the bed. Feather plumes explode from the mattress and float in the air, and grey cordite smoke conceals his face.

Suddenly the Marshal stands, firing his Colt - again and again. Bullets slam into Frank sending him crashing onto the opposite passage wall, slumping slowly to the floor, blood gushes from a wound in the centre of his face and one in his throat.

Strolling over the Marshal knows the shots would've alerted his friend and sliding along the passage wall, eases to where the stairs lead up from the main lobby. A woman sticks her head from around a room door but rapidly closes it on seeing him. The smell of fresh blood and gun-smoke envelope the air. Reaching the open landing, he peeps into the lobby. It's empty. Walking back into his room, he puts on his boots and reloads his gun. Returning to the corridor, he waits.

Entering Fort Smith, Sheriff Davis, his deputies - Percy and Warren - hear the gunshots from the hotel. They wait and listen and after a moment continue riding.

Heading from the saloon, Toledo, Will and Pat with guns drawn, march to the hotel. At the opposite end of the town Sheriff Davis fails to see them as they fail to see him and his deputies; the night concealing both men from each other.

"Pat, you go 'round tha back should that shitah try that way...," he pauses, "Will, we go through the front. Where tha shit is Frank? You told him to wait right, Pat?"

"Yeah boss but ah bet yah that was him, he's killed the shit already."

"Yah," Toledo doesn't sound too convinced.

Sheriff Davis heads to the local Sheriff's Office, "Looks like there's some excitement tinight."

Percy and Warren say nothing, sitting silently behind their boss, mounts slouching up the street.

"Ah'm checking in with the local Sheriff hif he's seeing anything. Ah'll..."

Just as he approaches the low brick building the sheriff's office door swings open and a burly man steps out, a double-barrelled shotgun in his big hands. Behind him three other men fan out on the sidewalk deputy badges twinkling in the lamplight shining along the walkway's wooden posts.

The man speaks, nodding in the posse's direction, "Mister, how can I help you?"

Sheriff Davis nods in return, "Sheriff, name's Davis, sheriff from Fayetteville, we're chasing Toledo and his gang, looks like they came this way."

The man shakes his head, "You sure Sheriff Davis, name's Wilson and I haven't seen Toledo or his gang pass this way. Ah didn't know he was anywhere near here." He points his weapon in the direction of the shooting, "Had a shooting over in tha hotel, going to check it out."

Sheriff Davis grunts, "Yeah, he killed a few of mah residents and robbed ah bank."

"I heard. Well, yah welcome to tag along. Sometimes we have these little incidents, nothing major."

Davis grunts again, unshackling his Winchester. The small posse dismounts and follows Sheriff Wilson and his three deputies towards Eddies *Emporium*.

9

He couldn't stop, not now. Snow engulfed his snowshoes and the flakes slap his face as if Mother Nature had a vendetta against him. Ploughing on, shielding his eyes, he knew his prey was near, how near he was not sure. Suddenly out of the blinding whiteness, a large dark figure emerged. Flexing his cold fingers, he gripped the butt of his pistol and like the weather about him, felt nothing but a chill. The cold finger of death would be doing the touching today.

Crouching, Will enters the hotel first, gun in hand. He glances quickly around the lobby, sees nothing, not even Eddie - the hotelier - is behind the counter. Starting up the stairs, Toledo follows.

Wooden steps creak and with every boot fall, his spurs make a soft tinkly sound. Eventually he reaches the landing and as he places a boot onto a wooden slat the Marshal suddenly emerges into the open and murmurs, "Will Harrison?"

"Yeah," Will answers, staring stupidly into a black hole of the Marshal's gun.

"Yah better come quietly Will."

The Marshal hears the shot before feeling it pass close by his head, its breath tantalising; a second bullet smashes the wall above his head. Diving back onto the landing, he fires; the first bullet crashes into Will's forehead. Dead centre. He tumbles backwards and tumbles down the stairs.

Toledo fires at the landing and glimpses at Will spread-eagled on the stairs, glassy eyes staring at the ceiling, blood spreading across the wooden floor. Reloading, Toledo snarls and fires.

Bullets splinter the banister and wall behind the Marshal and hidden from Toledo, he wriggles across the landing to the opposite side of the landing, firing sporadically as he goes. Rising unsteadily to his feet, he reloads, flinching whenever a bullet smashes into the adjoining wall.

"Marshal! Yah thare....!" There's a pause and Toledo yells again, "lissen yah shitah...yah ain't coming out alive, yah hear mi! You know who ah am?"

Smiling, the Marshal shoots and yells, "Toledo, my friend...yah tha one in the shit! Bah now, the Sheriff his on his way ovah here!"

A few more rounds slam into the wall above him and he returns fire. Suddenly, there's a commotion below; voices and more gunfire, none of which come his way. Listening, the noise move away, under the floorboards, through the building and to the rear. More shots and loud screams.

Racing along the passageway the Marshal bursts through the second floor rear door. Gunfire echoes between the close buildings, bouncing from one side to the next and pistol flashes in the tightly-walled alleyway light it up. Waiting for his eyes to adjust to the blackness, he sees a group of men, guns and rifles in hand, firing into the night. And in the distance, the sound of horse's galloping away, eventually disappears in the night.

10

The first Indian danced away, the knife he held in one hand floating back and forth; at times he'd toss it, never losing grip of its wooden handle. How long had he been living with them? Not long and he expected this test, it was a long time in coming but here he was sweat filming his brow and moccasined feet shuffling on the grass. If he made one wrong move, he'd be dead. He held the knife away from his body, its stainless steel dull in the late afternoon sunshine. He wasn't ready to die. Not today.

"You say what?" Sheriff Davis glares at the Marshal. "Ah don't need no Blacky telling me how to catch an outlaw. Screw that shit."

Ignoring the Sheriff the Marshal puts a spoonful of beans into his mouth. Sheriff Wilson watches both men, their respective deputies remaining in the saloon.

"Ah ain't telling you again Davis, ah have jurisdiction. There's no need toh go haftah Toledo. Ain't one of your men being dead satisfying enuff?"

"Yah mean Percy, rough shit," Sheriff Davis growls, "now you lissen niggah..."

The Marshal's stops eating and he looks hard at the Sheriff, "Ah hate being called a niggah and unless yah don't know am ah Deputy US Marshal...you know what that means, rite?"

"Ah don't give a rat's arse what that means niggah. You ain't stopping me fram following that shitbag!"

Wilson clears his throat as if to say something but the Marshal halts his comment with a hand. Rising unhurriedly to his feet, he walks to where Sheriff Davis stands and faces him; their noses inches away from away from each other.

The Marshal sighs, "Davis am done talking either you lissen tah me or get the shit out."

Davis snarls and suddenly throws a punch. The Marshal expects the swing and ducks, leading with his right. He hits the Sheriff in the midriff. Doubling over from the blow, he grunts. A quick left connects with his square jaw, busting his lips, spurting blood. He doesn't cut his assault and a flurry of punches follow, smashing into Davis' head and body. He falters fast-swelling as he tries to feel for the Marshal. Skilfully the Lawman dodges, hurling a telling blow to the side of the Sheriff's face. Staggering, nose broken and mouth bloodied, he topples, landing heavily on the dirt-packed floor.

"Like ah said...haf got jurisdiction," Setting his hat, the Marshal returns to his bowl of baked beans. "It's tha second time in has many days 'ave being called ah niggah...."

Miles from town Toledo crouches in the darkness. Hiding in heavy vegetation located in a deep wash, he flicks bullets from his gunbelt and reloads. Pat builds a fire a few feet away, a rough bandage wrapped around an upper arm; blood staining the material.

Pat says, "Tha other boys on their way boss?"

"Yeah!" Toledo growls, "ah don't know how long they'll take but ah want toh kill that damn Marshal," He angrily inserts shells into his rifle. "Ah want that shitting niggah dead."

Finished, he moves to his saddle pack. "We got toh ride Pat, ah want tah get toh Clarkesville by dawn."

11

The Marshal dismounts, studying the ground. The earth's trampled with track-marks; it's too difficult to read any sign. A bright day greeted his morning and like many before, a simple cup of hot black coffee and beef jerky was enough.

After a brief discussion his powers of persuasion forced both Sheriff Wilson and Davis to wait for his signal whenever he encountered Toledo, reluctantly they agreed. He was uncertain how that would happen since he'd be on the trail.

Staring towards a rising sun, he mutters, "Well Blaze, hif you were Toledo what would you do now?"

Blazes neighs, tossing her head.

"That's what ah think! He lost two men and Wilson and Davis said he was with one other. Where's tha rest? If I was him ah would wait out fah tha rest of the gang," He pats Blazes thick neck, "where would ah go, eh Blaze? He can't head north to Fayetteville, too obvious; go to Tulsa, over in Oklahoma...naw his prides bin slapped." Blaze's ears flicker. "So where would ah go? Where would Toledo go?"

Tugging the reins, he heads to Clarkesville.

Sheriff Davis paces the floor of his hotel room, a few times he sits on the bed before jumping to his feet. "Shit, ah can't deal with this bull!"

Grabbing his gunbelt from a bedpost he straps it around his waist and picks up his rifle, "Mr Toledo yah mine."

Swearing, he marches through the door.

Toledo rubs black stubble on his jaw. The reflection in the cracked mirror shows a face he barely recognises with craggy, crooked lines dispersing from eye corners and elongating across his forehead. Smiling, he wonders who the stranger is staring back at him.

Putting a glass tumbler to his lips, he gulps some whiskey. It burns. The saloon is nearly empty with just another three customers sitting at the far end of the bar, chatting with the barkeeper, the saloon's only customers.

Pat sits at a table by himself, a half-empty bottle of whiskey in front of him. Closing his eyes, Toledo massages his temples. The Deputy US Marshal in Fort Smith cost Will and Frank their lives and the posse nearly ended his own and Pats. *Shit ah Black Deputy US Marshal! Ah damn niggah!*

He drinks some more, pondering whether to lie low, wait on the guys or get some more cronies. Either way, doing it himself or with others, nothing and nobody is standing in his way to kill the Marshal. When they reach Fort Smith he knows the others will contact him, somehow. He smiles.

12

Children had never entered his mind, not when he was forever away. How could he be a good father then? Candace said what she needed to say and it felt heavy in his gut, like a solid rock was there but it he needed to go. The Tom Perrin Gang was on the rampage and somebody needed to stop them. He needed to stop them.

The Marshal waited a few days in the brush before journeying to Clarkesville, his ruse, to make Toledo believe his pursuers are no longer after him, giving him a false sense of security.

The town is quiet as he walks Blaze at the rear of the buildings; he feels at home in the dark but he still watches the gaps in-between the structures he crosses.

Strolling up an alley, he pauses and surveys the street. It's deserted. A number of tethered horses snort and otherwise than a couple of pedestrians, the town is still. Even the saloon is quiet – unusual for any western town. Smaller than Fort Smith, Clarkesville is a developing outpost with its single main road and few merchant building. He considers his next move before withdrawing into the shadows. *Mite as well bed down out of sight for tha nite.*

Four riders hitch their horses in front of the hotel just as soon as the Marshal vanishes. Their spurs jingling on the wooden floorboards, announcing their presence as one of them pushes open the door. A lamplight illuminates the heavy-set, heavily-armed men.

13

He had punctured something, he was sure. His breathing was ragged and he spat a globule of blood onto the trail. Removing a soaked red rag from his side, he looked at the wound. It was nasty. He wasn't sure if the knife had truly done any damage or the busted lip which caused him to spit blood. At least the dead outlaw straddled on the back of his saddle wouldn't know that.

The hotel room is crowded with the six men lounging on the few chairs or only bed while Toledo stands by the window looking out onto the street. Every man checks and rechecks his weapon. One man – Juaniez - sharpens a knife with a small grindstone.

"We ride in the morning," Toledo grins, nobody says anything. "Ah want tah fine that shitting niggah Marshal and that Springdale Sheriff."

A thin-faced man smiles, baring tobacco-stained teeth, "Where we heading boss?"

"Fort Smith."

Orange-red strips spread across a turquoise sky, the oncoming day pushing aside the black night as if announcing its presence to this part of the country. A lathered horse, legs dragging, head almost touching the ground, enters the town. Unloading himself from his nag and trudging over, Sheriff Davis seeks out the local lawman's office. Dust ingrains his rough face, chaps, jeans, shirt and coat and removing his gloves, he fits them into his gun-belt.

In the stable the Marshal fixes a saddle cinch and hearing the clip-clop of hooves on the streets hardened turf, takes Blaze's reins and walks out.

Toledo's leads the group down the stairs and stuck in his waistband, he packs an additional gun. Nobody speaks and every man carries his own saddle roll and rifle, holstered side-arms.

Pushing through the glass panel door, the street is quiet except for a man leading a horse towards the Sheriff's office and a shadow emerging from the stable. Sheriff Davis and the men exchange incredulous stares and standing in the shadows behind and to Sheriff Davis' right, the Marshal also recognises the men.

Toledo is the first to move, bringing the gun from his waist. "Davis!"

"Who tha?" shouts Sheriff Davis, reacting to his name being called as he searches for his Colt. It's in his hand quickly.

Toledo crouches, gun in hand, the rest of the gang scattering, rifles to their shoulders, hands pumping action, fingers squeezing triggers. One gang member screams, holding his gut as he buckles and falls to his knees.

Toledo's first rounds miss Sheriff Davis, kicking dirt at his feet. Another bullet slithers by his own back, tearing his shirt, taking flesh with it. On one knee, Davis fans his gun but a bullet ploughs into his shoulder. He shrieks, dropping onto his back, withering.

Walking into the open, the Marshal points his gun to the closest two gang members and fires. One man wails spinning away, bullet in his heart. The other man pitches sideways, half his head blown away. Projectiles whiz by the Marshal and spatter into the stables wooden boards. While on the ground shaking and holding onto his wound, another round hits Davis in the leg. He squeals again.

Aiming and firing, the Marshal walks calmly into the street, bullet spurts flicking dirt at his feet and ricocheting into the new morn.

"Niggah!" Toledo yells, quickly jumping to his feet, running to the opposite side of the street, firing as he went. Pat follows. A last gang member makes to run when two more of the Marshal's bullets slam into his side. He crashes head-first onto the wooden walkway floorboards.

Crouching, the Marshal chases after the outlaws and from within an alleyway shadow, someone fires. A bullet clips his ear, he grimaces but drowns his hurt; warm blood dribbles down his neck, soaking his shirt. The Marshal doesn't stop and returns fire.

In the pre-dawn shadow he pauses and leans against a building, panting as he reloads, breath racking his chest. Watching the alley ahead of him, he hears the neigh of horses. His blood his warm.

There's another shot, a bullet hits the wall above his head, wood chip splinters rain over him, moving, he fires again at the burst.

Somebody yells, "Shit! Ah'm hit!"

Running towards the shout, the Marshal hopes its Toledo and a projectile pulls at his shirt above his waist, a sudden searing pain causing him to grimace. Diving to the turf, he shoots back. Reaching the rear of a building, he sees hastily moving shadows and cursing, sprints to the stable and Blaze.

14

Blaze gallops and bent low over her neck the Marshal reloads. In front of him, Toledo's horse dances around the shrubs, through brush and trees while behind him, Pat slumps in his saddle, bumping with every stride of his nag. A large red blotch splays across his back and he groans loudly with every hoof.

Weakly, he hails his boss but Toledo fails to hear, focusing on driving distance between him and his pursuer. *Damn shit! Why doesn't he stop!*

"Boss!" Pat murmurs as he falls from his horse, crashing to the ground, screaming. Toledo reins in his mount, its gritted teeth chomping at the bit and taking one glance turns away, forcing his ride along the trail; he doesn't look back.

Dismounting, the Marshal walks over to where Pat lays face-down, groaning. Digging a toe into Pat's side, he turns him over, both his hands cover the spread of blood contrasting against his light blue cotton shirt. A red trickle crawls from a mouth corner.

Squinting at the figure over him, he whispers, "You shit!"

The Marshal squats, "Yup ah sure am!" Lifting Pat's hands he looks at the gut wound. "You bettah make peace with your God."

"Screw you niggah."

"Ah ain't the one dying friend...," The Marshal takes a poster from his pocket, unfurling it and reading the name on it.

"Pat Steel, huh? Shitty way tah go don't yah think?"

"Shit...," Pat coughs, red spittle splatters across his face and shirt.

"Ah wood wait till your dead Pat bury yah too but ah got tah go hafftah yah boss."

"...Yah'll never get him...," He coughs, "...he'll get yah first, yah see..."

"Sure we'll see...any final words?"

Pat has a coughing fit, "...Yeah, ah don't want tah wait for the vultures to pluck out mah eyes..."

The Marshal nods as he remounts and draws his gun, taking aim, he fires. The bullet smashes in-between Pat's eyes. They glaze and slowly he rolls onto his side; a sigh escaping his lips.

"Helluva way tah go." The Marshal mumbles, following in his foes tracks.

The bullet clips the Stetson from the Marshal's head. There's a boom seconds later, it bounces across the undulating hills and rolls away. A flock of scared scarlet tanager birds shriek as they ascended into the bright sunshine.

Throwing himself from his saddle while simultaneously grabbing his Winchester, he hits the dirt heavily and rolls into a shallow ditch. The earth spurts as more bullets spatter the ground above him, raining pebbles over him. Scrambling to a nearby bush he waits, watching for any further gunfire but there's only silence.

"Looks like he's dun running," He muses. "Where you at Toledo?"

A shot responds; the flash high on a ridge and off to his right, he knows better than to respond and crawls along the trench. In the humid heat perspiration clings to his clothes gathering dirt as he moves agonisingly to another clump of brush.

"Today is tha day," He mumbles, swatting a bead of sweat from his brow.

15

Her tongue caressed his. Its subtle flicks and twisting movements like a dance where they both needed to be in tune. Their embrace and longing was deep and true and he was in awe; the feeling of him inside her, the panting of her breath in his ear causing him to shudder like a lonely leaf on a naked branch; its softness, a warm breeze on a clear summer Arkansas day. He shivered again and gently biting into her neck, she groaned, withering under him in uncontrolled ecstasy. Their eyes. Closed. Hid the sweet blackness of universal togetherness and kissing her lips, he found her tongue again.

Concealed behind a hickory tree, Toledo surveys the valley floor below him. Firing once more, he crawls stealthily to another position, searching the terrain as he moves, trying to guess the Marshal's next move.

The air is still and with no breeze the pine trees remain immobile, their shadows caused by the sun, stretch over the hills and gullies.

On his hands and knees, rifle in hand, Toledo stares at the ravine where he last saw the Marshal, wild hydrangea is scattered at its mouth. Smirking, he fires, the bullet landing a foot from the Marshal's Stetson head.

He flinches. "The shitbag!" Removing his hat.

Searching the hill, he looks for the source - small stumps of short-leaf pine trees merging with fully grown pine and scrambling, he goes in the opposite direction.

Settling under the bush Toledo's cold eyes stare along his rifle towards the spot he feels the Marshal will appear. He needs only one shot.

The Marshal moves gingerly as shredded pine needles dig into his body, stinging him while he labours up the hillside, each clump of brush and shallow ravine helping to hide his arduous progress. During the rainy season the canyon's gullies would fill with water, turning the ravines into mini raging rivers. Fortunately, no rain has fallen in a few days. Daring not to breathe, he searches each tree, scouring the undergrowth, seeking out the outlaw.

Suddenly in front of him, sticking from a cluster of wild hydrangea, a pair of worn boots, heels sloping at an angle from the wearer's constant wear and walk; an attached spur dull in the sunny day.

Affixing the Winchester's stock to his shoulder the Marshal takes aim - he's certain he makes no sound and swears under his breath as Toledo's head snaps up; something has unnerved the outlaw as if a sixth sense alarm is triggered. Spinning from his position, he rolls, firing as he goes. Bullets smash into the tree beside the Marshal's head, one creases his scalp. He dives away, working his rifle's pump action, rolling for cover behind a pine tree stump.

More bullets thump into its trunk, splinters falling on him as he hugs the ground. Smiling icily, a blood trickle creeps down the side of his face.

"Com'on niggah!" Yells Toledo. "You die tah day fo sure shitah!"

They stop shooting and peeping around his barrier, the Marshal glimpses Toledo disappearing into the bush and quickly snaps off a few rounds. He follows, darting cover from cover.

Slithering into a dry gully, Toledo scares a desert rat, it scampers away into thicker brush. Crouching, he runs into a forest of pine trees that confront him and makes for the nearest tree, waiting, rifle ready.

The Marshal emerges, his shadow dark against the green of the forest, Toledo lets off a volley of shots.

The Marshal spins away and hides behind another tree. Squirming swiftly along the ground, he heads to Toledo's location. Then bent double, he runs quietly, panting he pauses, placing down his rifle while drawing his Colt.

Toledo glances around nervously, uncertain of his next move. Checking the rounds in his handgun, belt and rifle, he curses. His Winchester is almost empty. *Five rounds in mah belt and a fully loaded gun. Why doesn't this shitting niggah die? Where tha shit is he?*

He needs to get away.

As he moves, the Marshal steps from the shade, gun in hand.

"Toledo!"

"Shit! Niggah!"

Toledo runs towards the juniper, firing wildly before a loud click signals an empty rifle breech. Shots veer into the shadows beside the Marshal with one punching into his upper thigh. He staggers, grunting, half-turning, gun hand wavering.

Tossing the rifle aside, Toledo reaches for his handgun, "Niggah tahday it's you..."

Bent at the knees, fanning his gun, he fires once, twice, three times. Calmly, the Marshal crouches, pointing his Colt and fires.

A bullet shatters Toledo's collarbone, he screams, gun falling from a dead hand. A second projectile tears into his throat, throwing his head back and a third punctures the centre of his head, splattering red and grey brain matter onto the green forest floor. As the last gunshot reverberates over the hills, his scream dies in his throat. He's dead before the echo fades away.

Using his rifle as a crouch the Marshal staggers, limping to where Blaze is tethered. Toledo's horse is nearby munching on grass and leaning against his loyal ride, he unhitches a canteen, taking a swig. Sweat soaks his clothes, matting dirt on his skin and leaves and twigs, stick from his dreadlocks. Tearing strips from a spare shirt in his saddle roll, he makes a tourniquet and wraps it tightly around his leg. He grimaces with every move he makes. To the front and back of his thigh there's a large red spot. It is a through and through. His other wounds long dried and throbbing.

"Well Blaze looks like ah paid for this one." His horse neighs, tossing her head.

Sighing, he replaces the rifle into its scabbard and struggles to put his foot into the stirrup. Wincing, he launches up into the saddle and sits unsteadily, wrapping both his and Toledo's horse reins around the pommel. Gently he kicks Blaze's flanks and both horses trot towards the trail.

J.N. Nicholas

Bushwhacked!

Released July 2016

A brown mustang climbs wearily, its hooves clops steadily on the rocky earth. The barren ground strewn with few cacti and high boulders has a spattering of tumble grass, dotting the landscape like little clumps of forest. High above his head vultures circle expectantly as if waiting for something to happen to him or his mount. Gliding through the still air, he listens to them squawk with each turn, their shadows criss-crossing around him in an ever decreasing cycle as they continue to argue amongst themselves.

Smiling, he wearily removes his black Stetson, its grey with dust and wipes his forehead with the back of a dust-laden sleeve. He spits. The globule smacks the earth, heavily. He's thirsty. On his chest the tin U.S. Deputy Marshal's badge sparkles in the sunshine and feels unusually heavy.

He baulks. The heat on the top of his head causes him to rush and replace his inadequate reprieve. The material is inadequate. Smarting, he still feels the damning heat, even under the partial shade of his hat.

Dismounting, he grabs the water canteen strapped to the saddle's pommel. Splashing a few drops onto his fingers, he gently runs them across his cracked lips. He swears at the pain shooting its way into his hot brain.

Sprinkling some more of the precious liquid into a cupped hand, he places it under his trusted mount's snout. Tossing back its long head, the grateful horse neighs, glad for the nourishment. A large pink tongue slurps, emptying the little fluid.

"Sorry Blaze, this is 'all you getting right now," He rasps.

Tiredly he sits under his mount's shade checking her hooves. Two shoes are cracked. He swears again. A lame horse in the desert meant certain death. He wondered how far they had to go.

Removing his boots he inspects the soles. Run-down heels. Holes. He pushes a finger through one gaping wound. *No wandah mah bloody feet hurt*, he muses.

Releasing the 1861 Navy Colt from his side holster, he examines it for dust and wipes it clean with an oily gun rag retrieved from one of two saddle bags. He checks the action, its fine. Next, he snatches his two rifles from their scabbard; a single-shot Spencer carbine and a Henry repeater; going over the same procedure. There's no need for him to look at the nine inch knife in it sheath on his hip. It was recently sharpened on any rock he could find.

No sooner does he replace the weapons and wearily steps into a stirrup to mount, when there's a booming, rolling sound. A gunshot echoes throughout the nearby mountains, bouncing along the rock face.

About the Author

J.N. Nicholas currently resides in London, UK. An avid reader, he tried his hand a bringing to life an icon in American and African history.

He enjoys writing the Brass Hunter series and is sure it will be turned made into a television series one day.

J.N. Nicholas can be contacted at: baobabtreebooks@gmail.com or the website: www.baobabtreebooks.com.